RAINBOW magic ®

The Pet Keeper Fairies

For Tom Powell, with lots of love

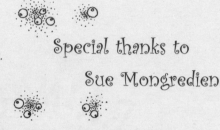

Special thanks to
Sue Mongredien

ORCHARD BOOKS
338 Euston Road, London NW1 3BH
Orchard Books Australia
Level 17/207 Kent Street, Sydney, NSW 2000
A Paperback Original

First published in Great Britain in 2006

HiT entertainment

A CIP catalogue record for this book is available
from the British Library.

ISBN 978 1 84616 168 1
9 10

Printed in Great Britain

Orchard Books is a division of Hachette Children's Books,
an Hachette Livre UK company

www.hachettelivre.co.uk

Georgia
the Guinea Pig
Fairy

by Daisy Meadows

illustrated by Georgie Ripper

ORCHARD BOOKS

www.rainbowmagic.co.uk

The Fairyland Palace

Wetherbury Village

Strawberry Farm

The Spring Show

Fairies with their pets I see
And yet no pet has chosen me!
So I will get some of my own
To share my perfect frosty home.

This spell I cast. Its aim is clear:
To bring the magic pets straight here.
Pet Keeper Fairies soon will see
Their seven pets living with me!

Contents

Farmyard Fun

"This must be one of the cutest animals in the whole of Strawberry Farm!" Rachel Walker declared, her eyes shining. She stroked the woolly lamb in her arms. "He's so cuddly!"

"And hungry, too," her best friend, Kirsty Tate, chuckled. She tilted up the bottle of milk she was holding to feed

the lamb, under the watchful eye of
a farmhand. "He's nearly finished
this already!"

"He's making me thirsty, just
watching him!" her mum said, as the
lamb drained the last few drops.

Rachel was staying with Kirsty's family for a week over the Easter holidays. This afternoon, they were having a great time at Strawberry Farm. They had already seen a troop of tiny ducklings venturing out for their first swim on the pond, and enjoyed a pony ride on a sturdy little brown Shetland called Conker. Then, when a farmhand had announced that he wanted some volunteers to help him hand-feed some of the lambs, Rachel and Kirsty had jumped at the chance!

Rachel put the lamb down carefully, and both girls watched him gambol off to join the other lambs in the field.

"I saw a sign for 'Pets' Corner' over there," Rachel said, with a meaningful look at Kirsty. "Shall we go there next?" Kirsty smiled at her friend, picking up on Rachel's message at once. The two girls shared a wonderful secret: they'd been helping the Pet Keeper Fairies of Fairyland all week! Nasty Jack Frost had kidnapped the Pet Fairies' seven magical pets and had taken them all to his ice castle. But the pets had managed to escape, and make their way into the human world. Yesterday, Rachel and Kirsty had helped Bella the Bunny

Fairy find her lost rabbit. And the day before they'd reunited Katie the Kitten Fairy with her missing kitten. So Kirsty knew exactly what Rachel was hoping: perhaps they'd find another magical pet today in the Pets' Corner!

"Sounds lovely, but I think I'll opt out and go for a coffee," Mrs Tate said. "Shall I meet you both back here at four o'clock?"

"Good idea," Kirsty replied, trying not to sound too enthusiastic. Much as she loved her mum, she and Rachel always had their very best adventures when they were alone! "See you later."

Mrs Tate went towards the tea room, and the two friends headed for Pets' Corner.

"Here we are," Rachel said as they entered an area surrounded by a small fence. "Keep your eyes peeled for any magical pets who might be here!" she added in an excited whisper.

The girls began looking at all the rabbits and guinea pigs in their hutches and runs. Every animal had a little sign

outside its cage, telling visitors its name and favourite food.

"Ahh, this rabbit is called Albie, and he likes carrot tops and brussel sprout peelings," Kirsty read aloud, peeping in at the fluffy grey rabbit. "Hello, Albie!"

"Rosie the guinea pig likes sunflower seeds and lettuce leaves," Rachel read, further along the row of hutches. "Millie, her sister, likes sliced apple. And Carrot, Rosie's baby, likes carrots... Oh!"

Kirsty looked up. "What's wrong?" she asked.

Rachel was crouching down and peering into one of the runs. "There are supposed to be three guinea pigs in here — Millie, Rosie and baby Carrot," she told Kirsty. "But the baby guinea pig is missing!"

ROSIE, MILLIE & CARROT
Rosie likes sunflower seeds and lettuce leaves. Millie, her sister, likes sliced apple, and Carrot, Rosie's baby, likes carrots and banana sk...

Kirsty hurried over. "Oh, dear, look," she said. "The cage door's open a crack — Carrot must have escaped!"

Out of the corner of her eye, Rachel

suddenly spotted a flash of fur behind the
hutches. She turned to see
a small orange and white
guinea pig squeezing
under the wooden fence.
"That must be Carrot
over there," she cried.

Kirsty fixed the cage door firmly shut,
then jumped up to look. "Oh, no – he's
heading for that field of sheep!" she
said, pointing.

Rachel looked anxious and headed off
after the little guinea pig. "He's too
young to be out on his own," she said.
"We've got to rescue him, Kirsty!"

Magic in Mid-Air!

Kirsty and Rachel clambered over the wooden fence surrounding the field of sheep and hurried after the guinea pig, who was now scampering busily towards a tree on the far side of the field. But both girls stopped and stared in disbelief when the guinea pig reached the base of the tree, for instead of stopping, or swerving around the tree, the little animal simply ran straight on up the trunk!

"I didn't think guinea pigs could do that!" Kirsty gasped. "I'll go after him, in case he gets stuck." Kirsty clambered up into the tree and picked her way from branch to branch until she was within arm's reach of the little guinea pig, who was watching her curiously.

20

"Hello," Kirsty
said in a soft
voice, reaching
out towards
him. As she did
so, the guinea pig
twitched his nose and
backed away playfully.

Kirsty stretched out her hand a little
further. "Come here, little Carrot,"
she said coaxingly. Again the guinea
pig backed away, and Kirsty thought
she glimpsed a whiskery little smile on
his face as he did so!

"I'm imagining things now," Kirsty
said to herself. She inched a little
further along the branch and then
leaned out in an effort to reach the
guinea pig. Just as her fingertips were

about to touch Carrot's fur, he jumped
right off the branch…and scampered
merrily away through the air!

Kirsty nearly fell out of the tree in
surprise. "Rachel, look!" she cried
excitedly, scrambling back down to
the ground.

Rachel felt a delicious thrill of excitement as she realised what was happening. "That's not Carrot, the farm guinea pig," she laughed. "It must be Georgia the Guinea Pig Fairy's magic pet!" She and Kirsty had met all the Pet Keeper Fairies in Fairyland. "I wonder where Georgia is."

At that very moment, the girls suddenly heard the sound of cheerful singing above them, and looked up to see Georgia herself swooping towards them on the back of a blackbird.

"Georgia!" Rachel cried, waving at the pretty fairy.

Georgia waved back cheerily as the
blackbird perched near the girls on
a branch of the tree. She had short
black hair and she wore a tan-coloured
top and suede skirt, both edged with
a fringe of turquoise beads and tassels.
She smiled as she slipped off the
blackbird's back and thanked him for
the ride. The blackbird chirruped
a merry reply and fluttered away.

Georgia flew over to Rachel's shoulder, her gauzy wings shimmering in the sunlight. "Hello, girls," she said, in a clear, silvery voice.

"We were looking for a lost guinea pig called Carrot," Kirsty explained eagerly. "But we found your magic pet instead, Georgia!"

Georgia twirled in mid-air excitedly when she heard that. "I thought he was somewhere near here!" she declared, looking around. "Oh, Sparky, hello!" she called, seeing the little orange and white guinea pig trotting along in mid-air. "I've missed you so much!"

Rachel smiled as Sparky squeaked joyfully in reply to his fairy owner and began scampering towards her. Meanwhile, the little fairy was listening to Sparky's eager squeaks. "He says that he's been looking for Carrot, too," she told the girls. "And—"

But before Georgia could translate any more of Sparky's message, one of the sheep who'd been grazing nearby suddenly leaped up on its hind legs. To everybody's amazement, the sheep then produced a butterfly net, swept it through the air and captured Sparky!

"Hey!" Kirsty yelled. "What's going on?"

"That's not a sheep," Rachel called out in horror, seeing a long green nose poking out from the creature's woolly face. "It's a goblin in disguise!"

Goblins Undercover

A gleeful cackle floated through the air as the goblin ran across the field with Sparky trapped in the butterfly net.

"Oh, no!" Kirsty cried. "What are we going to do now?"

"I'll turn you into fairies so we can all fly after him," Georgia said quickly, waving her wand over the girls.

A stream of glittering turquoise sparkles
swirled out from the tip of her wand
and whirled around Kirsty and Rachel.
In an instant, both girls shrank down
to become tiny fairies.

Rachel fluttered her
shimmering wings,
enjoying the feeling
of being as light as air
as she floated off the
ground. Being a fairy
was just about the best thing

in the whole world,
but now the girls
had work to do!
"Let's follow that
sneaky goblin!"
she cried, zooming
through the air after him.

"Don't worry, Sparky, we're coming!"
Kirsty added, following Rachel.

But as they flew over the field of
sheep, several more sheep jumped up on
their back legs and began swiping at
Kirsty, Rachel and Georgia. More
goblins in sheep disguises!

"Now they're chasing us!" Rachel
warned, looking back over her shoulder
to see the goblins racing after them
with butterfly nets in their hands and
nasty grins on their faces.

"Fly higher," Georgia urged the girls. "Don't let them catch you, too!"

Kirsty, Rachel and Georgia flew up out of reach of the goblins as they chased after the one who'd caught Sparky. He ran into a big old barn, and they all zoomed in after him.

It was very dark inside the barn, and at first the three friends couldn't see very much in the gloom. But then Georgia muttered a few magic words and the turquoise tip of her wand suddenly glowed

brightly, like a glittering blue torch.
"Sparky, where are you?" she
called softly, fluttering over a
stack of hay bales to look
behind them. Kirsty and
Rachel were also
flying around the
barn, hoping to
catch a glimpse of
the guinea pig.
Suddenly, Sparky
gave a couple of
high-pitched squeaks,
and Kirsty, Rachel and
Georgia flew towards
the sound at once.
The magic pet's squeaks
seemed to be coming from
somewhere near the barn door.

Unfortunately, just as the girls and Georgia approached the door, the other goblins ran into the barn, and cheered with delight to see the three fairies hovering in front of them, caught off-guard.

"Catch them!" one of the goblins urged, swinging his net around in an attempt to scoop up the fairies.

"Oh, no, you don't!" Georgia cried, as she and the girls soared upwards away from the goblins.

Kirsty managed to dodge one goblin who made a grab for her, but the tallest goblin of all now had her in his sights. As Kirsty flew up, the goblin swished his butterfly net down – and Kirsty was caught in its mesh!

"Help!" she cried, beating her wings frantically as she tried to fly free.

"Ha!" the tall goblin smirked, putting a warty green hand over the top of the net. "You're my prisoner now!"

Trapped!

Georgia grabbed Rachel's hand and
pulled her up to a small, broken
window above the barn door, just as
the goblins swung the door shut with
a thump.

"What are we going to do?" Rachel
asked Georgia, her heart beating wildly
as they squeezed through the hole in

the window.
"The goblins
are holding
Kirsty prisoner!"
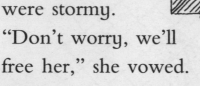
Georgia's eyes
were stormy.
"Don't worry, we'll
free her," she vowed.
"We need to think of a way to rescue
Kirsty and Sparky fast!"

Rachel and Georgia fell silent as they
both thought hard. They could hear the
goblins chortling triumphantly inside
the barn.

"A guinea pig and a fairy," one of
them crowed. "What a haul!"

"Jack Frost is going to be really
pleased with us today," another added,
sounding smug.

Then Rachel and Georgia heard
a scraping noise as the goblins slid
the bolt across the barn door.

"We'll sit tight until those other two
fairies have gone," a goblin muttered.
"Then we'll take this fairy and the
guinea pig back to Jack Frost's castle."

Rachel thought it was horrible to
hear the goblins gloating. She perched
on the window frame, racking her
brain. "Georgia, do you
think Sparky might
be able to magic
himself into
an elephant or
something, and
charge the door
down?" she suggested
after a few moments.

Georgia shook her head vigorously. "Sparky won't be able to use any magic," she told Rachel. "None of the magic pets can when they're afraid." She frowned in concentration. "We'll have to make the goblins want to leave the barn somehow," she went on. "Maybe we could tempt them out with something nice to eat?"

Rachel grinned as a brilliant idea suddenly popped into her head. "Or we could scare them out," she said eagerly. "Georgia, do you think you would be able to magic up the sound of an angry bull?"

"Of course," Georgia replied. Then she beamed as she realised what Rachel was plotting. "Of course, the sound of an angry bull who's just been woken up by noisy goblins will be just the thing to drive those goblins out of the barn!" she whispered with a mischievous chuckle.

Rachel nodded happily. "The barn is so dark that the goblins will never know that it's only fairy magic they can hear," she added.

Georgia and Rachel grinned at each other, and fluttered down to the ground.

"Let's give it a try," Georgia said. "The sooner we free Kirsty and Sparky, the sooner we can find little Carrot."

She waved her wand, sending more turquoise sparkles swirling around Rachel. As soon as the magic fell upon her, Rachel grew back to her usual size.

Then Georgia pointed her wand at the barn doors and they shimmered for a few seconds with a magical turquoise light. "There," she whispered to Rachel. "I've used magic to hold the door shut, so even if the goblins unbolt it, they won't be able to come out until we let them."

Rachel smiled. "And we'll only let them out when they promise to hand over Kirsty and Sparky," she whispered back. "Brilliant, Georgia!" Then, with a wink at the smiling fairy, Rachel raised her voice. "Beware of the bull?" she said, as if she were reading aloud from a sign. "I wonder if those goblins know they're stuck in the barn with Farmer Tom's mean old bull. Phew!

He's a bad-tempered creature, way too crazy to be out in the fields." She laughed loudly. "I wouldn't like to be in there if the bull wakes up!"

Rachel glanced up at Georgia, who was now hovering outside the window above the barn door. With a wave of her wand, the little fairy sent a stream of magic all the way into the darkest corner of the barn.

Snort! Grunt! CRASH! A terrible grunting and bellowing started up where Georgia's magic had landed, complete with a thunderous hoof-stamping sound.

Georgia flew back down to perch on Rachel's shoulder, trying not to laugh out loud at their clever trick.

Rachel pressed her ear to the barn door to listen to the goblins.

"Whose stupid idea was it to come in here anyway?" one of them hissed nervously.

"Farmer Tom's crazy b-b-bull sounds really a-a-angry!" another goblin stuttered.

Rachel and Georgia heard the sound of the bolt being pulled back, and then one of the goblins tried to push the door open, but, of course, Georgia's magic was holding the door firmly shut.

"You're trapped in there," Rachel couldn't resist telling the goblins, "with Farmer Tom's mad bull!"

"Maybe the bull will make a nice pet for Jack Frost," Georgia suggested sweetly.

"Hey, let us out right now!" a goblin demanded, thumping on the door.

"I don't think so," Georgia replied in her silvery fairy voice.

Then, she zoomed up to the window and waved her wand again, sending more magic into the barn. Immediately, the ferocious bellowing of an angry bull started up inside, but this time it sounded even more bad-tempered.

"Oh, dear, all that shouting seems to have made the bull even angrier!" Georgia remarked sorrowfully.

The goblins hammered wildly on the door in panic. "Let us out right now!" they chorused.

Girls and Goblins Agree

"You let Kirsty and Sparky go, and then we'll let you out of the barn!" Rachel shouted to the goblins.

There was a moment's silence. "We can't go back to Jack Frost and say we've let another of those pesky pets slip through our fingers," Rachel heard a goblin whisper.

"First we messed up the kitten kidnap, then we bungled the bunny bagging. If we come back today without the guinea pig—"

"We can't go back without the guinea pig," another goblin interrupted. "But how about if we..."

Rachel pressed her ear as close to the barn door as possible, but the sneaky goblins were talking so quietly now that she couldn't hear what they were plotting.

"The fairy can go, but the guinea pig's staying with us!" a goblin voice announced after a moment.

Rachel looked at Georgia in dismay. She hadn't been expecting that response. "What shall we say?" she whispered.

"Let's agree, and then at least we know Kirsty's safe," Georgia replied. "Perhaps one of you will be able to grab Sparky as the goblins come out of the barn?"

Rachel nodded. "OK," she hissed. Then she turned back to the barn door.

"It's a deal," she shouted to the goblins. "Set Kirsty free!"

There was an anxious moment or two as Rachel and Georgia waited to see if the goblins were plotting a trick of their own, but then Kirsty zoomed out of the window and flew down to join them, smiling with relief.

Georgia waved her wand and turned Kirsty back into a girl.

Rachel hugged her tightly. "Are you all right? Were they mean to you and Sparky?" she asked.

"I'm fine," Kirsty said. "And so is Sparky. He's being very quiet, but he isn't hurt."

A peevish knocking came from the other side of the barn door. "A deal's a deal," one of the goblins yelled. "Open up before this crazy bull finds us."

Georgia pointed her wand at the doors.

"Now, we're going to try and grab the goblin who's got Sparky, OK?" Rachel whispered to Kirsty.

Kirsty nodded. "He was standing behind the others, at the back," she told Rachel quietly. "Ready when you are, Georgia."

Georgia waved her wand. The barn doors glittered with bright blue light again and then burst open. The goblins immediately raced out of the barn.

"Quick! Before the bull starts chasing us!" one of them shrieked.

Kirsty and Rachel made a lunge for the last goblin who was clutching Sparky, but their hands closed around empty air as he dodged them nimbly and sprinted away across the field.

"He's getting away!" cried Rachel in despair.

Kirsty looked around frantically for something she could use to stop the goblin.

Suddenly, she spotted an old coil of rope just inside the barn. "Georgia, could you magic that rope into a lasso for me?" she asked quickly.

"Yes," the fairy replied, waving her wand in a pattern that sent turquoise fairy dust spiralling along the length of the rope. The frayed old rope immediately turned into a lasso and flew straight up into Kirsty's hand.

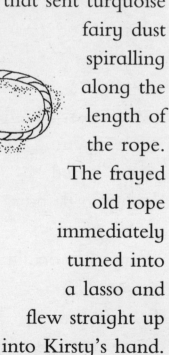

Kirsty swung the loop of the lasso around her head, keeping her eyes firmly fixed on the goblin who had Sparky. Then she launched the lasso straight at him.

The girls held their breath as the lasso flew through the air. It seemed to be heading a little wide, but Georgia quickly pointed her wand at it, and the lasso shone with blue magic and veered back on course towards the goblin. The loop of rope fell right over the goblin's head and caught tight around his middle, pinning his arms by his sides.

The goblin tried to keep running,
but the rope pulled itself magically out
of Kirsty's hands and wound itself
around the goblin's legs, until he had
to stop.

"Got him!" Kirsty cheered jubilantly.

Odd One Out

"Help!" the lassoed goblin yelled to his friends, but they were all far too busy running away from the imaginary bull to notice.

Rachel and Kirsty walked calmly over to the struggling goblin. Sparky, who was still in the goblin's hands, squeaked a welcome.

"Come here, Sparky,"
Rachel said, gently
lifting him out of
the goblin's fingers.
Sparky squeaked
even louder when he
saw Georgia fluttering in mid-air, and
with a twitch of his nose, he jumped
up towards her. As he was leaping
through the air, he shrank to his usual
tiny size and Georgia picked him up
happily for a cuddle.

"Hey! What about me?" the goblin
shouted crossly, still
tangled in the rope.

Georgia smiled at
him. "Don't worry,
the magic will
wear off the lasso
soon," she assured
him. "In a couple
of hours, or so,
you'll be free…"

"A couple
of hours?" the
goblin groaned.

Georgia winked at Kirsty and Rachel
as they began making their way back
towards Pets' Corner. "It will only be
a couple of minutes, really," she
whispered, with a laugh.

Sparky started squeaking urgently, and suddenly Georgia looked worried. "Of course!" she cried. "We must find poor little Carrot! I'd almost forgotten about him."

Rachel looked at her watch. "It's a quarter to four already," she said. "Kirsty, we have to meet your mum in fifteen minutes. We don't have long to find Carrot."

"Then I'll turn you back into fairies," Georgia said, waving her wand briskly. "That way we can all fly around and look for him. Let's split up and meet back at Carrot's hutch in five minutes."

Fairy-sized once again, Rachel and Kirsty zoomed off in different directions, searching for the little, lost guinea pig. Kirsty checked out the play area, the cow barn and even popped through the windows of the gift shop, while Rachel hunted around the pig pen, the duck pond and the stables.

But there was no sign of Carrot anywhere.

"I don't understand it," Georgia said when they met up with her again five minutes later. "Where could he be?"

"We should go soon," Rachel said ruefully, "but I can't bear to leave the farm without knowing that Carrot's safe!"

Kirsty suddenly pointed ahead to where a mother hen was being followed by her line of chicks. "Wait a minute," she said, narrowing her eyes. "That's an odd looking chick at the end of the line!"

Rachel looked over to where Kirsty
was pointing, and then giggled in
relief. The last 'chick' in the line was
not yellow and fluffy, like its fellows.
It was a small, carrot-coloured
guinea pig!

"Carrot's adopted a new family,"
Georgia chuckled. "How sweet!"

Sparky scampered over to Carrot and squeaked at him conversationally. Georgia, Rachel and Kirsty watched as Carrot looked at Sparky, then back at the chicks, as if he was working something out. Then he rubbed noses with Sparky and squeaked a reply.

Georgia grinned. "He says he's enjoyed being part of the hen family, but thinks he ought to go home now," she translated. "And we think so, too, little Carrot!"

Georgia checked that nobody else was
in sight, then waved her wand over
Rachel and Kirsty,
turning them back
into girls. Kirsty
went over and
picked up Carrot.
"Come on," she
said gently. "Let's
take you back
to your hutch."
As soon as Kirsty had
placed Carrot back in his hutch,
Rosie and Millie — Carrot's mum and
aunt — rushed over and squeaked at
Carrot excitedly. Then all three of
them rubbed noses together, and
Carrot nestled against Rosie, looking
very content.

Georgia waved her wand to make sure that the cage door was tightly shut. "So there'll be no more going back to the hen house, OK?" she said to Carrot, with a smile.

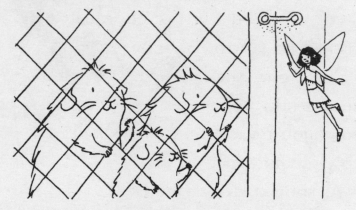

Then she picked up Sparky, and turned to the girls. "It's nearly four o'clock, you'd better go," she told them. "And we should fly back to Fairyland, too, Sparky – where I'm going to make sure Jack Frost never gets anywhere near you again!"

Sparky nuzzled Georgia's arm and she stroked him gently. "Thank you for everything," she said to Kirsty and Rachel. "And Sparky says thank you, too."

Kirsty and Rachel hugged the tiny fairy goodbye, and gave Sparky a gentle stroke. Sparky squeaked goodbye to the girls, and then squeaked in the direction of Carrot's cage. A volley of squeaks came back in reply, as if the farm guinea pigs were calling out their goodbyes too.

And then, with
a burst of
turquoise sparkles
that fizzed and
glittered in the
afternoon sunlight,

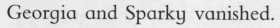

Georgia and Sparky vanished.

Rachel and Kirsty watched as the air rippled with a strange turquoise shimmer and then was still once more.

"There you are, girls!" came a voice, and Rachel and Kirsty turned to see Mrs Tate walking towards them. "Have you had a nice day?"

"Great, thanks, Mum," Kirsty replied with a smile. "Wasn't it, Rachel?"

"Oh, yes," Rachel agreed. She grinned broadly as she noticed a pot of sunflower seeds, some sliced apple and a whole pile of carrot sticks in the guinea pigs' cage.  She felt sure the food was a gift from Georgia; it definitely hadn't been there before. "Today's been absolutely magic!" Rachel sighed happily.

Win Rainbow Magic Goodies!

There are lots of Rainbow Magic fairies, and we want to know which one is your favourite! Send us a picture of her and tell us in thirty words why she is your favourite and why you like Rainbow Magic books. Each month we will put the entries into a draw and select one winner to receive a Rainbow Magic Sparkly T-shirt and Goody Bag!

Send your entry on a postcard to Rainbow Magic Competition, Orchard Books, 338 Euston Road, London NW1 3BH. Australian readers should email: childrens.books@hachette.com.au New Zealand readers should write to Rainbow Magic Competition, 4 Whetu Place, Mairangi Bay, Auckland NZ. Don't forget to include your name and address. Only one entry per child.

Good luck!

RAINBOW magic ®

The Pet Keeper Fairies

Georgia the Guinea Pig Fairy has got
her pet back! Now Rachel
and Kirsty must help

Lauren the Puppy Fairy

Puppies on Show

"Look at that marrow, Kirsty," Rachel
Walker laughed, pointing at the large
green vegetable on the display table.
"It's nearly as big as I am!"

Kirsty Tate read the card propped
against the marrow. "It's won a prize,"
she announced, "for Biggest Vegetable
at the Wetherbury Spring Show."

There were other enormous vegetables
on the table too, and the girls stared
at the giant-sized carrots and onions.
There were also huge bowls of
daffodils, tulips and bluebells. The best

flower displays had won prizes too.

"This is great!" Rachel declared, as she finished her candyfloss. "I wish we had a Spring Show back home."

Rachel was staying in Wetherbury with Kirsty for the Easter holidays, and the girls had spent the whole afternoon at the show. The field was crammed with stalls selling home-made cakes, biscuits and jams, and there was a tombola, a hoopla and a coconut shy, as well as pony rides and a huge red and yellow bouncy castle. Rachel and Kirsty had really enjoyed themselves.

"I think we've been round the whole show," Kirsty said at last. "Mum and Dad will be here to pick us up soon."

"Shall we have one last look at our

favourite stall?" asked Rachel eagerly.

"You mean the one for Wetherbury Animal Shelter?" Kirsty said with a smile.

Rachel nodded. "I want to see if they've found homes for those four puppies."

"I hope so," Kirsty said. "They were really cute! And talking of pets…" She lowered her voice so that she wouldn't be overheard. "Do you think we might find another fairy pet today?"

"We'll just have to keep our eyes open!" Rachel whispered in a determined voice…

Have you checked out the

RAINBOW
magic®

website at:

www.rainbowmagic.co.uk

Look out for the Fun Day Fairies!

THEA THE THURSDAY FAIRY
978-1-84616-191-9

WILLOW THE
WEDNESDAY FAIRY
978-1-84616-190-2

TALLULAH THE TUESDAY FAIRY
978-1-84616-189-6

MEGAN THE MONDAY FAIRY
978-1-84616-188-9

SARAH THE SUNDAY FAIRY
978-1-84616-194-0

SIENNA THE SATURDAY FAIRY
978-1-84616-193-3

FREYA THE FRIDAY FAIRY
978-1-84616-192-6

Out now!

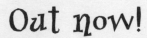